GOODBYE
to
YESTERDAY

THE
Discovery
PART 1 *of* 6

A Lancaster County Saga

GOODBYE to YESTERDAY

WANDA E. BRUNSTETTER

BARBOUR
PUBLISHING

© 2013 by Wanda E. Brunstetter

Print ISBN 978-1-61626-085-9

eBook Editions:
Adobe Digital Edition (.epub) 978-1-62029-690-5
Kindle and MobiPocket Edition (.prc) 978-1-62029-689-9

All scripture quotations are taken from the King James
Version of the Bible.

This book is a work of fiction. Names, characters, places, and
incidents are either products of the author's imagination or
used fictitiously. Any similarity to actual people, organizations,
and/or events is purely coincidental.

Cover design: Kirk DouPonce, DogEared Design
Cover photography: Steve Gardner, PixelWorks Studios

Published by Barbour Publishing, Inc., P.O. Box 719,
Uhrichsville, Ohio 44683, www.barbourbooks.com

*Our mission is to publish and distribute inspirational products
offering exceptional value and biblical encouragement to the masses.*

Member of the
Evangelical Christian
Publishers Association

Printed in the United States of America.

To all my Amish friends who live in Pennsylvania.
I appreciate your friendship and hospitality.

Thou wilt keep him in perfect peace,
whose mind is stayed on thee:
because he trusteth in thee.

Isaiah 26:3

CHAPTER 1

Bird-in-Hand, Pennsylvania

Would you like another piece of bacon?" Meredith Stoltzfus asked her husband, barely able to look at his grim expression as he sat across from her at the breakfast table.

"No thanks," Luke mumbled. The sparkle was gone from his beautiful turquoise eyes, and there was no joy on his bearded face. They'd only been married a little over a year, and already the thrill seemed to have worn off. At least for Luke it must have. Meredith had been so sure about his love for her during their courting days and throughout the first eight months of marriage. But now Luke's attentiveness had been replaced with worry and defeat. When Luke lost his job at the nearby furniture store, everything had changed. Oh, not at first. Luke had been optimistic, saying he was sure the economy would turn around and that he'd either get hired back or would find another job where he could use his woodworking skills. But that had been six months ago, and he was still out of work, as were some of the other Amish men the store had let go. Luke hardly talked about it anymore, but Meredith knew it was eating at him.

"Would you like some more juice?" Meredith asked, reaching for the pitcher of apple juice.

He shook his head. "I'm fine. Haven't finished what's in my glass."

"No, you're not fine, and I wish you would talk about it instead of sitting there, staring at your plate."

He shrugged. "There's nothin' to talk about."

Meredith sighed. Lately, all she had to do was look at her husband to know he was depressed. Luke's stance was no longer confident. He walked slightly hunched over, with a look of uncertainty and doubt. Gone was his open-minded manner, replaced by edginess and impatience. Luke's folks had offered to help out financially, but Luke had turned them down. Since Luke's dad had sold his bulk food store and worked part-time for the man who'd bought it, Luke's folks were getting by okay, but they weren't well off. Meredith's parents wanted to help as well, but they had seven other children to raise—all still living at home. And Grandma Smucker had moved in with them two years ago, after Grandpa died of a heart attack, so she, too, needed their financial support. On more than one occasion, Meredith had suggested that she look for a job, but Luke wouldn't hear of that. He insisted that it was his job to provide for them.

Meredith, trying to be optimistic, was thankful that while Luke had been working at the furniture store, he'd put some money into a savings account he had started even before he'd met her. They'd been given some money from several people who'd attended their wedding, and that had gone into the bank as well. Since losing his job, Luke had sold some of his handcrafted projects at the local farmers' market, as well as at a few gift shops. That had helped some; but for the most part, they'd been living off their savings. That money wouldn't last forever, and Meredith feared they might be unable to meet all their financial obligations if Luke didn't find a job soon.

She sighed. Being forced to pinch pennies had put a strain on their marriage. When Meredith and Luke had first gotten married she'd been convinced that the love between them could withstand any hurdle. Now, she wasn't so sure. To make things more complicated, Meredith felt pretty sure she was pregnant. She'd sometimes been irregular but had never missed two consecutive months. After her appointment with a local midwife next week, she'd know for sure. She hadn't told Luke, though, and felt apprehensive about doing that before she was certain. He was already uptight about their finances, without worrying about the possibility of having another mouth to feed in about six months.

But if the midwife confirmed Meredith's suspicions, she'd have to tell Luke soon because it wouldn't be long before she'd start to show. If Luke could just find another job, all their worries would be put to rest.

She cleared her throat. "Uh, Luke, I need to do some shopping today, and I was wondering— would it be okay if I buy some paint for the spare bedroom next to ours?"

Luke's eyebrows furrowed as he pulled his fingers through the ends of his thick blond hair—so blond it was nearly white. "Using our money for groceries is one thing, but paint will have to wait till I'm working full-time again."

Meredith clenched and unclenched her fingers. *What would he say if he knew that spare room I want to paint is for the baby I believe I'm carrying? Should I go ahead and tell him right now, or would it be better to wait?* "I know we have to be careful with our money," she said, "but paint shouldn't cost that much."

"It costs more than I want to spend right

now." Luke drank the rest of his apple juice and pushed away from the table. "Now, if we're done with this discussion, I need to go out to the barn."

"But Luke, I really would like to paint that room because—"

"I said no, Meredith," Luke said firmly. "We can't afford to do any painting right now. The spare room can stay like it is for the time being. There's no need to paint anyways, since we're only using it for storage. Until we get on our feet again, we should leave well enough alone."

"But Luke, if you knew—"

"Mir sin immer am disch bediere iwwer eppes." He frowned. "And I'm gettin' tired of it."

"It does seem like we're always arguing about something," she agreed, "and I don't like it, either."

"Then let's stop arguing and talk about something else." Irritation edged Luke's voice.

"You can be so *eegesinnisch* sometimes," she muttered, looking away.

"I'm not being stubborn; I'm being practical. And as far as I'm concerned, this discussion is over!"

Goodbye *to* Yesterday

Luke grabbed a dog biscuit and went out the back door, letting it slam behind him. Meredith flinched. It wasn't right for them to be quarreling like this. It wasn't good for their marriage, and if she was pregnant, it certainly wasn't good for the baby. She would never have imagined that their lives could change so drastically in such a short time.

Meredith jumped up, moving quickly to the kitchen window, watching through a film of tears as Luke tromped through the snow to fuss with his dog, Fritz, before going into the barn.

She ran her fingers over the cold glass. *I wish Luke would communicate with me as easily as he does with his dog.*

Sometimes Meredith wondered if it would be better for her to not even talk to Luke unless it was absolutely necessary. It was ridiculous to be thinking this way, especially since up until recently they'd always discussed things and made important decisions together. But wouldn't it be less stressful to keep quiet than to quarrel with him all the time?

A year ago, those thoughts would have

never entered her mind. How was it that they were either behaving like total strangers or snapping at each other these days? When they were newly married, with their future spread out before them, Meredith had been full of hopes and dreams, and every day had been blissful. Now the discouraging job outlook was swallowing Luke up and affecting every aspect of their marriage.

Despite it being a nice idea to spruce up the terribly drab spare bedroom, Luke was probably right about not spending the money on paint with their finances so tight. Paint wasn't that expensive, but in Luke's eyes, it may as well cost a million dollars. Even a few cans of paint were a luxury they really couldn't afford. If the midwife confirmed Meredith's suspicions, then maybe she could start moving some boxes up to the attic. That would need to be done anyway, before it became a baby's room.

She reached for the teapot simmering on the stove and poured some hot water over a tea bag in a cup. While it steeped, she cleared the breakfast dishes and ran water into the sink. Then, blowing on the tea, she took a cautious sip. The warm liquid felt good on her parched throat. For now, she would forget about painting the room and stop adding to the anxiety her husband already felt.

Lord, she silently prayed, *please help Luke find another job soon, and while we're waiting, help us learn how to cope.*

"Sure wish I could find another job," Luke mumbled as he crunched his way through the snow toward the barn. He and Meredith hadn't argued at all until he'd gotten laid off. Now it seemed like all they did was argue. *Guess it's mostly my fault, but I can't help being fearful that we'll lose everything if I don't find something soon. Maybe I should quit being so stubborn and let Meredith look for a job. Maybe she'd have better luck finding one than I have.*

Luke had made good money working at the furniture store, but he'd been one of the newest men hired, so when things got tight, he was the first to go. He guessed during these hard economic times that people were buying less furniture, even the finely crafted kind. Luke had applied for several other jobs in the area, but no one seemed to be hiring. Even though he'd sold a few of his handcrafted items, that income wasn't enough to fully support them. This whole situation sure was discouraging!

"How are you doin' there Fritz, ole boy?" Luke asked, hearing his German shorthaired pointer bark out a greeting and feeling glad for the diversion. "Don't worry, I hear ya." Entering the pen, he petted the head of his beloved companion and bird dog. Good ole Fritz. Luke loved that faithful critter, and he was glad Meredith loved the dog as much as he did.

Last winter, Meredith had insisted on bringing Fritz into the house, where she felt he would be warmer. Luke would have preferred to keep the dog outside in the kennel like he had when he was still living at home. But after a while, Meredith convinced him to let Fritz become a part-time house pet. Those times that he was allowed to stay inside, Fritz would lie right by their feet while Luke and Meredith ate popcorn or played board games. At night while they slept, Fritz was like their guardian angel, lying on the floor by the foot of their bed, watching over them and keeping the house safe from intruders. So now only on rare occasions did Fritz stay outside in his kennel at night.

Luke squatted down and scratched the soft fur behind the dog's ears, while Fritz gazed back at him with trusting brown eyes. Fritz was beautifully marked. His head was a solid liver color, and his body was speckled with spots and patches of liver and white. Fritz was affectionate and gentle with everyone. He'd no doubt be good with their children when Luke and Meredith started a family. Luke didn't have that in mind when he'd first purchased Fritz, of course, but it just so happened that the breed produced not only excellent hunting dogs but also good family pets.

Most times, Fritz accompanied Luke when

he went to visit his parents. Even Mom and Dad's barn cats tolerated the dog when he'd bound over to greet them in his happy-go-lucky manner. Sometimes, it seemed as if they actually enjoyed his company, when they'd lie down beside him on a bed of straw and take a nap.

"Do you want to play fetch?" Luke asked.

Fritz tilted his head to one side, as though understanding exactly what his master meant, and then, like a streak of lightning, he took off across the yard.

How can dogs be so smart that way—understanding what people are saying to them? Luke wondered. *Sometimes I think that critter's smarter than me.*

"Find a stick, boy!" Luke commanded, watching Fritz run around with his nose to the ground.

In no time, Fritz returned with a small branch that Luke could throw for him to retrieve. If Luke let him, the energetic dog could run for hours. Then he'd flop on the floor and sleep.

From the time Luke bought Fritz, when he was an eight-week-old puppy, he and the dog had bonded. Fritz followed Luke everywhere. He'd had an easy time training Fritz, too, and there wasn't anything the dog wouldn't do for him. So loyal and willing to please his master, Fritz would sit in anticipation, eagerly waiting for Luke's next command. Good ole Fritz was the best bird dog ever. At least Luke thought so. With hardly any training, Fritz tracked and flushed pheasant, rabbit, or grouse as well as any spaniel or retriever.

As he and Fritz played fetch, Luke looked toward the house. He and Meredith had been so excited after their home was built. Luke had beamed with satisfaction when his wife thanked him for all the hard work he had done in constructing the home. Their wedding ceremony had taken place at Meredith's childhood home, but afterward, everyone had come back here to celebrate and share the wedding meal. The fall day had been warm, so they'd set up long tables in the yard to accommodate the large crowd, as well as the variety of food and desserts that everyone enjoyed. It had been a wonderful day, starting their new life together surrounded by family and friends. Luke had felt good about their roomy two-story home that he hoped would one day be filled with their children's laughter.

"Come on, boy. That's enough for today," Luke finally called, clapping his hands after having given his dog a small workout. He wished he could spend more time with Fritz, but he had chores that needed to get done. "I see your water dish is frozen," Luke said, whacking the ice onto the ground and then refilling the bowl with fresh water.

Fritz wagged his docked tail and anxiously sniffed Luke's hand.

"*Jah*, here it is. You know I always have a treat for ya." Luke grinned as Fritz gently took the dog biscuit he offered him.

Seeing that Fritz was relaxed and content with the biscuit between his paws, Luke stepped into the barn and quickly shut the door. It was bitterly cold, and the wind howled noisily, finding its way through the cracks in the walls. He'd be glad when spring came, and he hoped he would have a job by then.

Goodbye *to* Yesterday

It's a good thing it's only me and Meredith right now, Luke thought as he stepped into his horse's stall. *If we had a family to feed, I'd be even more troubled than I am right now.*

Luke was glad they didn't owe any money on their house. He'd built it with the help of friends and family, and all of the building materials had been purchased by Grandpa Stoltzfus, who had since passed away. Despite the lack of a mortgage payment, property taxes still needed to be paid come spring. Taxes alone were high enough, but so far, they'd been manageable. But like nearly everything else, they were supposed to increase this year, and Luke hoped their savings account would still have enough money to cover the bill when it came due. If he could just sell a few more of the wooden things he'd made. Of course, that money would be nothing compared to the wages he'd earned at the furniture store.

Luke thought about Meredith's request to buy paint. He hated saying no to her. If he could, he wouldn't deny his wife anything. Normally, Meredith was quite understanding.

For that, and many other reasons, Luke felt blessed. She wasn't the type to ask for much, and buying some paint was really no big expense—that is, until now. It may as well be the moon she was asking for. And while she only wanted to paint the room, most home projects inevitably led to more, so for now, painting or any other home improvement just wasn't a necessity.

Luke knew Meredith was concerned about their finances, too. He also knew she kept herself extra busy around the house so she wouldn't fret so much about him being out of a job. That's how Meredith had always dealt with things. She hadn't slept well since he'd been out of work, either. Many a night, he'd wake up and discover her standing in front of their bedroom window, staring out at the moon. Well, Luke was worried, too, and it was taking a toll on him. He'd become irritable and impatient, often snapping at Meredith for no reason. He owed her an apology and planned to do that as soon as he returned to the house.

Shaking his thoughts aside, Luke fed and

groomed their two horses and then cleaned out their stalls. Taffy was Meredith's horse, and rightly named. The mare was the color of deep molasses taffy, with a mane and tail that was almost black. Luke's horse, Socks, was appropriately named, too. All four of the gelding's feet had white patches that looked like socks, and while pulling their buggy, it appeared as if he was showing them off with each prancing step he took.

When Luke was done with his chores in the barn, he decided to walk down the driveway to the phone shack to check for any messages.

Inside the small building it was so cold and damp that Luke's teeth began to chatter, and when he blew out, he could see his breath, heavy in the air. Blowing on his hands for some warmth, he clicked on the answering machine to listen to the first message.

"Hello, Luke. This is your uncle Amos out in Middlebury, Indiana. I was talkin' to your *daed* the other day, and your name came up. You see, I'm plannin' to retire from my headstone-engraving business, and I was wondering if you'd be interested in coming out to Indiana as soon as possible to learn how to run the business. I'm sure you'd catch on fast. And if you don't have enough money to pay for all my tools and equipment right now, you can give me half down, and the rest after you've learned the trade and have started making money. In case you're wondering, I don't expect you to move to Indiana. Just thought you could come here to learn the trade; then when you return home and the tools and supplies have been sent, you can open your own business there. There's another fellow in my area doin' this kind of work right now, so it's a good time for me to sell out, and I'd like it to be to a family member. Give me a call soon and let me know if you're coming."

Luke dropped into the folding chair inside the phone shack and listened to the message again. He wanted to make sure he wasn't hearing things. Uncle Amos had been engraving names on headstones for a good many years and was now ready to pass the trade along to a family member. Since he had no sons to take over his trade, this was a golden opportunity for Luke. Perfect timing, one might say.

"Thank You, Lord. This is surely an answer to our prayers," Luke said aloud. He knew of only one other Amish man engraving headstones in eastern Pennsylvania, but he lived clear up in Dauphin County, so Luke was sure he'd get plenty of business right here in Lancaster County, and it would be a benefit to the community.

Luke was tired of being pulled lower and lower into a valley of unanswered questions, and he wanted more than anything to stand up straight, feeling safe and secure about their future. Uncle Amos's offer was a chance for a new start, and he couldn't let it slip through his fingers. The only problem now was that Luke didn't know how he could justify to Meredith drawing money out of their savings to pay his uncle half the amount he would need to purchase the equipment. He'd just told her they couldn't afford to buy paint for the spare bedroom. How would she take the news that he wanted to withdraw money from their dwindling bank account to learn a new trade he wasn't even sure he'd be any good at? Not only that, but would Meredith be okay with him being gone for a few weeks until he learned this new skill?

$\mathcal{C}$ HAPTER 2

$\mathcal{G}$uess what, Merrie? I have some really good news!" Luke shouted, bursting into the kitchen with an upbeat grin.

Meredith turned from the sink, where she stood drying the dishes. The look of enthusiasm on her husband's face made him seem like a different person than the one who had abruptly walked out the door a short time ago. "What's the good news?" she asked. Luke even seemed to be standing a little taller.

"I just came from the phone shack, and

there was a message from my uncle Amos. He's decided to sell his headstone-engraving business, and he wants me to buy it!" Luke's grin stretched across his face, and his turquoise eyes twinkled like they used to before he'd lost his job. "This is the answer we've been looking for, Merrie. Jah, it's an answer to our prayers!"

Meredith stood with her mouth gaping open.

"Well, what do you think? You look kind of stunned," Luke said, moving toward her. "Aren't you excited? Don't you think this is the break we've been hoping for?"

She drew in a couple of deep breaths, hating to throw cold water on his plans. "I am a bit bewildered, Luke. I'm sure your uncle means well, but doesn't he realize you don't know anything about engraving names on headstones? And we can't afford to buy his business, Luke. We don't have a lot left in savings."

"Don't worry, Merrie. At first I was shocked, too, and I had the same questions running through my mind that you have right now. But Uncle Amos is gonna teach me all that I need to know, and he said I can give him just half of the money for his equipment now and pay the rest after I get the business going. Once I'm on my feet and start bringing in an income, we should be able to pay him in no time a'tall. Uncle Amos's business has always done well, so I'm sure it'll bring in a steady income." Luke stopped talking long enough to draw in a quick breath. "It may sound kind of morbid to say this, but sad as it is, people are always dying, so this type of business isn't likely to fail."

Meredith grimaced. "You're right, that does sound morbid, and just so you know—I'm not in favor of this."

"Why not, for goodness' sake? I need a job, and the way things are now, we could use up all our money just trying to stay afloat." Luke's expression turned serious. "It's hard to face failure, Meredith, and I don't want that for us. Can't you see that I need this opportunity for a new start right now?"

"I understand all of that, but I like living near our folks, and if we had to move to Indiana

I know we'd both really miss them." She clasped his arm. "Luke, this is our home."

He shook his head. "We won't have to leave. I'll be buying Uncle Amos's equipment and starting my own business right here."

"But you're a woodworker. I would think you'd want to find a job doing what you do best and what you love to do. Could you really be happy doing something other than woodworking?"

"Well, I—"

"It'll be hard to learn a new trade, and how are you going to? Is Amos going to come here to teach you?"

Luke shook his head. "He wants me to come there."

"When?"

"As soon as possible, and I thought I'd see about getting a bus ticket right away. I shouldn't be gone more than a few weeks, and I'd really like your blessing on this new venture." He gave Meredith a hug. "I need to do this for us—for our future. I can't go on like this anymore, wondering and worrying about if and when our money will run out and where the next dollar's gonna come from."

"But it's January—the middle of winter, Luke. The roads between here and Indiana are probably bad, and I doubt you could find a driver who'd be willing to take you there right now."

Luke clasped her shoulder. "Aren't you listening to me, Meredith? I don't plan to hire a driver. I'll make the trip by bus. After Uncle Amos teaches me all that I need to know, I can figure out the best way to get the equipment I'll be buying sent back to Pennsylvania." He leaned down and nuzzled her ear. "Come on, what do you think? Are we in agreement about this? I feel like God is handing me this chance, and I can't let it go by without at least trying. Surely you understand that, don't you?"

Meredith hesitated. Then she gave a slow nod. "All right, Luke, if that's what you think is best." *Although I'm really not sure it's the right decision for us,* she silently added.

He kissed her cheek. "I'm going back out to the phone shack and give Uncle Amos a call so he'll know what we've decided. After that, I'm gonna call Mom and Dad, and give them the good news. Do you want me to call your folks, too?"

"No, that's okay. I'll let them know later today."

"I'll bet everyone from both our families will be as happy about this as we are." Luke kissed Meredith's other cheek. "There's no need to worry now. It'll all work out, you'll see. Oh, and Merrie, there's one more thing."

"What's that?" she questioned.

"I know I've been kinda hard to live with lately, and. . ." He paused and reached for her hand. *"Es dutt mir leed."*

Tears pooled in her eyes. "I've been difficult at times, too, and I'm also sorry."

Luke gave her a tender hug. "Okay, I'm goin' out to the phone shack now."

Meredith couldn't help but smile as she watched her husband hurry out the back door. He had a real spring to his step, and he definitely stood taller, with no hint of a slouch. So quickly his once-defeated expression had turned to one of hope. Despite her misgivings, Meredith truly wanted to have faith that this trip to Indiana would be the answer to their prayers.

"I'm gonna hitch Socks to the buggy, and then I thought I'd go over to see Seth and tell him about Uncle Amos's offer," Luke informed Meredith when he returned to the kitchen after leaving a message for his parents. She was sitting at the table with her Bible open, deep in concentration, with her head bowed slightly and a wisp of strawberry-blond hair sticking out the back of her stiff white head covering. "Would you like to go along?" he asked, placing his hand on her shoulder. "You can visit with Dorine."

Meredith looked indecisive but then nodded. "It has been awhile since I spent any time with her."

"Since your folks' house isn't far from the Yoders', maybe we can drop by there after we're done visiting with Seth and Dorine," Luke suggested.

"That's a good idea. I haven't called them yet, so we can tell them in person about your uncle's message."

Luke smacked his hands. "All right, then! I'll put Fritz in his kennel and get my faithful *gaul* hitched to the buggy so we can be on our way."

"This is a nice surprise," Seth said when Luke entered his barn and found him dragging a bale of hay across the floor toward the horses' stalls. "What brings you by here today?"

Luke smiled and moved closer to Seth. "I got some good news this morning and wanted to share it with my best friend."

Seth beamed. "What is it? Did you find another woodworking job?"

"Actually, I think I have found a job, but it's got nothin' to do with wood. I'm gonna be engraving headstones."

Seth's bushy brown eyebrows lifted high on his forehead. "Huh?"

Luke quickly explained about his uncle's phone message and said he'd be going to Indiana as soon possible.

"Now that is surprising news!" Seth thumped Luke's shoulder and grinned. "Seems like our prayers have been answered."

Luke nodded. "That's how I see it, but I'm not sure Meredith agrees."

"How come?"

"She's concerned about us drawing more money out of our savings, and she's also worried about me traveling in the dead of winter."

Seth leaned against the gate on his horse's stall and raked his fingers through the ends of his chestnut-colored beard. "Guess most women would be worried about that. I know for sure that my *fraa* would be." He chuckled. *"Ich memm zu hatz alles as me; fraa saagt."*

"I take to heart all that my wife says, too," Luke said, "but sometimes she's wrong about things. I'm sure Meredith will be fine with this once I'm back from Indiana and have begun making some money in my new trade," he added, feeling more confident by the minute.

"Jah, that's right, and I'll bet you will succeed if you just go for it." Seth clasped Luke's shoulder and gave it a squeeze. "Sometimes you have to give up things you thought you wanted before you reap the rewards of the things you least expected."

"It's nice to see you. Now, sit yourself down, and we'll have a cup of tea," Dorine said when Meredith entered her warm, cozy kitchen.

"*Danki*. I think that's just what I need on this chilly morning." Meredith removed her dark woolen shawl and hung it over the back of a chair. "Oh, it feels so good in here," she said, rubbing her hands together after a chill shivered through her body.

"Can you stay awhile? It's been some time since we've had a good visit." Dorine's pale blue eyes twinkled as she motioned for Meredith to sit down. "The little ones are taking their morning naps, so we can have some uninterrupted time together."

"Luke's out in the barn, talking with Seth, so we'll stay until he's ready to go." Meredith took a seat. "Yum. . .something sure smells good."

"I've had a pot of vegetable soup simmering on the stove for about an hour," Dorine said after she'd poured them both a cup of tea. "I thought it would taste good on a chilly day like this. You and Luke are more than welcome to stay and have lunch with us if you like."

"The soup sounds good, but we probably won't stay that long. We're planning to stop by my folks' place yet." Meredith sighed deeply before blowing on her tea.

"Is everything all right?" Dorine asked, pushing a stray wisp of dark hair under the side of her white head covering. "Those wrinkles I see in your forehead make me think you might be worried about something."

"Jah, just a bit." Meredith waited until Dorine had joined her at the table, and then she told her about the offer Luke had received from his uncle.

"That's good news," Dorine said. "Since

Luke needs a job, it's certainly an answer to everyone's prayers."

Meredith took a sip of tea then set the cup on the table. "That's what Luke thinks, too, but I'm not so sure."

"You don't think Luke should buy his uncle's business?"

"I do have some concerns."

"But Luke needs a job, and this sounds like the solution to your financial problems."

"I know it does, but it's going to take a big chunk of our savings for him to buy his uncle's equipment—even if he only pays for part of it now and the rest once he starts making money from the business."

"He shouldn't have any trouble earning that money after he begins engraving headstones here." Dorine's tone was optimistic.

"Maybe." Meredith took another sip of tea, letting the warm liquid roll around on her tongue. She wished she could be optimistic about this like her husband and best friend seemed to be, but something deep inside her said Luke's trip to Indiana was a big mistake. If the new business didn't do well, then what? They'd still have to pay for the equipment and would be even worse off than they were right now.

"If it were me, and my husband was out of work, I'd be thrilled about the opportunity that's being offered to him," Dorine said.

"I do hope it all works out, but. . ." Meredith's voice trailed off as she struggled with her swirling emotions.

"Is there something else bothering you?" Dorine asked, placing her hand gently on Meredith's arm.

Meredith nodded. "Luke's planning to travel by bus to Indiana, and with it being the middle of winter right now, I'm worried about the weather and road conditions."

"I'm sure the roads will be fine, and even if they're not, those bus drivers are used to driving in all kinds of weather."

"I suppose you're right." Meredith paused. "It'll be hard being away from Luke, though. In the fourteen months we've been married, we've never spent even one night apart."

"Why don't you go to Indiana with him?"

"I'd like to, but I don't think we should spend the money for an extra bus ticket. Besides, Luke will be busy learning his new trade, so I think it'll be better for both of us if I stay home." Meredith was tempted to tell Dorine about her suspected pregnancy but didn't think it would be fair to say something to her friend when she hadn't even told Luke. Truth was, another reason Meredith didn't want to go was because she'd been so tired lately and didn't think she could tolerate a long bus ride.

"I know it'll be hard having Luke gone, but it shouldn't be for too long, and you can always stay with your folks."

Meredith shook her head. "Mom and Dad have enough on their hands with my seven siblings and Grandma Smucker all living under one roof."

"You're welcome to stay here with us while Luke is gone," Dorine offered, getting up to stir the soup. "Of course, our two little ones can get kind of noisy at times."

"I appreciate the offer, but I'm sure I'll be fine by myself. Besides, I'll have Fritz to keep me company, and as you said, Luke shouldn't be gone too long." Meredith smiled, feeling a little better about things. "You know the old saying 'Absence makes the heart grow fonder.' When Luke gets back, we may even have a new appreciation for each other."

ℰ HAPTER 3

ℳonday afternoon, Meredith paced nervously between the living-room window and the fireplace. Pacing was a habit she'd acquired at a young age. It didn't really help anything, but it made her feel better to be doing something other than just sitting and fretting. Luke would be leaving tomorrow afternoon, and all day she'd been struggling with the urge to beg him not to go. It wasn't just the money he'd taken out of their savings that worried her, nor was it how much she would miss him. What bothered Meredith the most was the bad weather she'd heard they were having in northern Indiana. Even here in Lancaster County it was cold, and there was already some snow on the ground. How would the roads be between here and there? She'd be worried sick until Luke arrived safely at his uncle's place on Wednesday evening. *Indiana. . . Oh my, it seems so far from here,* she thought with regret.

Meredith went to the desk across the room and opened the bottom drawer, where Luke kept a map of the United States. Placing it on the desk, she studied the distance between Lancaster, Pennsylvania, and South Bend, Indiana. Looking at it this way made it not seem so far, and by bus it was only a day plus a few hours away. Maybe she was making too much of this whole thing.

I need to stop fretting and trust that God will take care of Luke, Meredith told herself as she put the map away. She stepped up to the window and focused on the beautiful red cardinals eating from the feeders in their front yard. The scene reminded her of what the Bible said in Matthew 6:26: "Behold the fowls of the air: for they sow not, neither do they reap, nor gather into barns; yet your heavenly Father feedeth them. Are ye not much better than they?"

If God takes care of the birds, then He will take care of me and Luke and help us with all our problems. I just need to believe and trust that He will.

Meredith placed one hand on her stomach. *Should I go ahead and tell Luke that I think I'm pregnant, or would it be better to wait until he gets back from Indiana?* She took a seat in the rocker near the fireplace. The rhythmic motion of the chair soothed her nerves somewhat as she thought about the situation.

She looked forward to being a mother and was sure Luke would be a good father. But if she told him now, he would probably worry about her while he was gone, and she didn't want that. If the midwife confirmed on Wednesday that she was pregnant, then she would surprise Luke with the news when he returned home. Fortunately, there hadn't been any signs of morning sickness yet, so she was sure he had no idea she might be carrying his child. Besides her missed monthlies, Meredith's only symptom was fatigue, but Luke hadn't seemed to notice that, either. Perhaps it was because he had so much else on his mind.

Meredith decided she was comfortable sticking with her decision to wait. If she was pregnant, the news would make quite a homecoming for Luke. The idea of them becoming parents made her feel somewhat giddy. By July they could possibly be a family of three.

But what if she wasn't pregnant? Maybe her fatigue and missed periods were caused from undue worry and lack of sleep. She'd heard of that happening to some people, and with the stress she'd been under since Luke lost his job, it could definitely have affected her monthly cycle.

Meredith leaned her head against the back of the chair and closed her eyes, feeling drowsy all of a sudden. It was exhausting, fretting about everything and wrestling with the fear of Luke traveling in the dead of winter, not to mention them having to spend time apart. Meredith had to keep reminding herself that this was only temporary; it was just a few weeks. Why, then, did that feel like forever to her?

I just have to get through these next few weeks, and then nothing but happiness will follow, she told herself. It sounded convincing enough. Now if only she could believe it.

She was thankful Luke had taken the time to finish up a few odd jobs that needed to be done around the house before he left. She didn't want to worry about problems with the house while he was gone. Luke was in the basement right now, fixing a leaky pipe, and Fritz was lying quietly by Meredith's feet. Maybe she had time for a short nap to ease her mind and help her relax before it was time to visit Luke's folks for supper this evening.

Poor pup, Meredith thought as Fritz grunted and changed positions. *I'll bet that dog's going to miss Luke almost as much as I do.*

❧

When Luke finished working on the leaky pipe, he glanced around the basement to see if there was anything else that needed to be done. Last year the basement had flooded during a hard rainstorm, but Luke had taken care of that by waterproofing the walls, so he was sure it wouldn't happen again. On Saturday, he'd cleaned the debris and ice from all the gutters and chopped extra firewood, enough to last until he was back home again. The wood was stacked close to the house so Meredith wouldn't have to go far to fetch it. Luke felt good that those tasks had all been completed.

He was anxious for tomorrow to arrive so he could be on his way to Indiana. The sooner he left, the quicker he'd get back home. But he hated to leave his beautiful wife. He wished Meredith could go with him, but they'd agreed it would be best if they didn't spend the extra money for a second bus ticket. Besides, once he got to his uncle's place, he'd be so busy learning his new trade that he wouldn't be able to spend much time with her, anyway. He was sure the time would go by quickly, and he'd soon be back, ready to start his new business.

Luke had seen the sadness in his wife's eyes and knew she still had some misgivings. But she was putting up a brave front and seemed to have accepted the idea. He hoped she had, because he was almost certain that buying his uncle's business was the right thing to do. And no matter how difficult it would be in the beginning, he was determined to make a go of it. When he started earning money at his new profession, Meredith would see that, too.

Luke gathered up his tools. He needed to head outside and hitch Socks to the buggy; then he would shower and change clothes before he and Meredith went to his folks' house for supper. Mom had insisted they come, saying it would be a few weeks before they saw Luke again. She'd also reminded him to bring Fritz along. Because he was the youngest of five boys and the only son living in Lancaster County, Mom tended to hover over him a bit. Two of Luke's brothers, Daniel and David, lived with their wives and children north of Harrisburg in the small town of Gratz. John and Mark, the two oldest brothers, and their families had settled in a newly established Amish community in western New York.

Luke had wondered for a while if he should move there, too—especially after he'd lost his job. He was glad he hadn't, because with this new opportunity, he and Meredith shouldn't have to worry about their finances any longer. He'd finally have what he hoped would be a secure job, and he wouldn't have to consider moving somewhere else and starting over, like some of the others in their community who'd lost their jobs had done.

Luke trudged up the basement stairs and went out the back door to get Socks out of his stall. It wouldn't be good for the horse to get lazy while he was gone, so he'd asked Seth to come by a couple of times and take the horse out for a run. Socks was a bit spirited, so Luke didn't want Meredith to take him out alone. If she needed to go somewhere, she was better off with Taffy, her easygoing mare, pulling the buggy.

"Are you about ready to go?"

Meredith jumped at the sound of Luke's

voice, followed by Fritz's excited bark. "Oh, sorry. Guess I must have dozed off." She yawned and stretched her arms over her head. "Are you done in the basement?"

He gave a nod. "I finished up with the leaky pipe some time ago. Then I went out to hitch Socks to the buggy, came back in here, and took a shower."

"I must have been sleeping so hard that I didn't hear you come in." Meredith stood and smoothed the wrinkles in her dark blue dress. "What time is it? I hope we're not running late."

"We're fine," Luke said. "Mom probably won't have supper on the table for another hour yet."

"Even so, I think we should go now, because I want to help her with the meal."

Luke pulled Meredith into his arms and kissed her gently. "You're so kind and considerate. No wonder my folks love you like their very own *dochder*."

"I love them, too, and I'm happy if they think of me as a daughter." Meredith gave him a tight squeeze then turned toward the kitchen. "I'll get my outer bonnet and shawl, along with the chocolate shoofly pie I made to take for dessert tonight, and then we can be on our way."

"Mmm. . .I hope you made an extra pie."

"I made two, and I'll take them both, so I'm sure there will be enough for you to have two pieces if you like."

He grinned. "I can hardly wait."

Meredith made a mental note to be sure she baked a chocolate shoofly pie for Luke's return home. She would also make his favorite meal of baked pork chops, mashed potatoes, creamed corn, and pickled beets.

"Did you feed Fritz?" Meredith asked when the dog barked again.

"Nope. Mom said we should bring the pup along and that she'd have something for him to eat."

"Do you hear that, pup? We're going for a ride." Meredith laughed when Fritz ran to the door, circling with excitement.

Luke leaned over to the pat the dog's head.

Meredith smiled. She was relieved that things weren't as strained between her and Luke as they had been for the last several months. The last thing she wanted was to send him off on a sour note.

ℰ CHAPTER 4

𝒜s Meredith and Luke headed down the road toward his folks' house, the only things breaking the silence were the steady rhythm of the buggy wheels and an occasional whinny from Socks. Luke was already missing Meredith, and he hadn't even left yet. He looked over at her, knowing she was probably feeling the same way. "What are you thinkin' about, Merrie?" he asked, reaching over to touch her arm.

"Oh, nothing, really. Just enjoying the ride."

From the backseat, Fritz leaned forward,

poking his head between them, yapping with excitement and then panting with his tongue hanging out of his mouth.

Meredith giggled. "I'll bet if Fritz could talk, he'd be asking: 'Are we there yet?' "

Luke nodded and clicked his tongue to get Socks moving a little quicker, watching the horse's feet prance higher as if in a dance. Then he looked over his shoulder at Fritz and said, "Don't you worry, boy. We're almost there."

When Luke pulled his horse and buggy up to his folks' hitching rail a short time later, he turned to Meredith and said, "Why don't you go on up to the house while I put Socks away in my daed's barn? Fritz can come with me. I'm sure he'll want to play with the barn cats before we go in for supper."

"All right, I'll get the box with the pies."

"Don't worry about that. No need for you to lug the box while you trudge through the slippery snow. I'll bring it up when I come in."

"Danki." Meredith stepped down from the buggy, and as she made her way to the house, Luke unhitched his horse and led him into the barn while Fritz followed close behind. Dad was feeding his horse, Dobbin, in the stall closest to the door.

"Wie geht's?" Luke asked, leading Socks into the stall next to Dobbin's.

"With the exception of the arthritis in my knees, which always acts up during cold weather, I'm doin' pretty well," Dad replied, limping over to greet Luke and then giving Fritz a few pats before the dog explored the barn. "How are things with you?"

"I'm fine, but I'll be even better once I get back from Indiana with a new trade I can use."

The wrinkles around Dad's brown eyes lifted when he smiled. "Jah, and I'm sure that's gonna be the case."

Luke grabbed a brush from the shelf overhead and started brushing Socks. The horse had worked up a pretty good lather on the ride over here and needed to cool down.

"Sure am glad you and Meredith could come over for supper this evening." The look in Dad's eyes, peeking at Luke over the top of his metal-framed glasses, revealed the depth of his love. "Your *mamm* and I wanted the chance to say goodbye before you leave tomorrow."

"We appreciate the invite." Luke blew out his breath in one long puff of air. "I have a favor to ask of you, Dad."

"What's that?"

"I'm worried about my fraa bein' alone while I'm gone, and even though I know Fritz will be there to watch out for Merrie and keep her company, I was wondering if—"

Dad held up his hand. "Say no more. You're not to worry, Son. Your mamm and I will check on Meredith often, and I'm sure her folks will do the same."

"I appreciate that." When he finished brushing his horse, Luke leaned on the half wall between the two horses' stalls and watched as Dad groomed Dobbin. "I haven't mentioned this before, but there's been some tension between me and Meredith since I lost my job at the furniture store."

"Figured that might be the case, and your mamm's noticed it, too." Dad limped around to the other side of Dobbin and started brushing the horse's flanks. "Money—or the lack of it—can have a way of causing problems between a man and his wife."

Luke gave a nod, looking toward the commotion in the back corner of the barn and then grinning when he saw his dog and two of Dad's barn cats cavorting with each other. Fritz stood barking at one of the smaller cats that was crouched on a bale of hay, as though ready to spring. The kitten started swatting at Fritz's nose, while another cat jumped at the dog's short tail.

Turning his attention back to his dad, he said, "Things are already somewhat improved between me and Meredith, and once I get back from Uncle Amos's place and begin making some money, I'm sure they'll be even better."

Dad smiled while stroking his mostly gray beard. "I'm glad my *bruder* offered to sell his business to you, Luke. I think you'll learn the new trade quite easily 'cause you've always been able to catch on to new things. Just remember, you'll be good at whatever you do as long as you give it your best."

Luke gave a nod. "I'll probably miss not working with wood anymore, but I guess I can still make a few things on my own, even if I'm not employed at a job where I can put my carpentry skills to use. And who knows? Maybe once Uncle Amos teaches me how to engrave headstones and I start earning an income from it, I may like the new profession even better than woodworking. Whatever happens, though, I'll try to remember your words and do my best."

"I'm sure it will all work out, Son." Dad stopped grooming Dobbin long enough to give Luke's shoulder a reassuring squeeze. "It never hurts to learn another skill. Leaving is the hard part, but once you're home, you'll be glad you made the decision."

"Thanks, Dad. Talking to you always makes me feel better about things."

Dad smiled; then he put the brush away, slipped out of his horse's stall, and closed the door. "Let me give your horse some food and water, and we'll head up to the house and see if your mamm's got supper ready." He grinned at

Luke. "Don't know about you, but I'm feelin' pretty *hungerich* right now. And how about you, Fritz? Are you hungry?" he asked, pointing at Luke's dog.

Woof! Woof! Fritz bounded over, forgetting all about the cats for the time being.

Luke chuckled and thumped his stomach as it growled noisily. "Guess it's pretty obvious that I'm hungry, too."

"It was nice of you to invite us over for supper this evening," Meredith said as she helped her mother-in-law, Sadie, set the table.

Sadie smiled, her hazel-colored eyes fairly twinkling. "We're glad you could come."

Luke's mother was always so cheerful. In fact, Sadie's radiant smile was contagious, and at the age of sixty-seven, she still had the cutest little dimples. Just being around her made Meredith feel at ease.

"I think Fritz was glad he was allowed to come with us. In fact, I believe the pup loves coming over here almost as much as we do." Meredith had nicknamed Luke's dog "the pup" soon after she'd married Luke.

"He sure is a good dog." Sadie grinned as she placed a pitcher of water on the table. "That first night when the puppy was brought home, Luke slept on the floor next to the box he had fixed up for Fritz. After that, they were inseparable."

"I can understand. I've gotten pretty attached to Fritz as well."

"So, tomorrow's the big day, jah?" Sadie asked.

Meredith nodded. "Luke's pretty excited about learning a new trade from his uncle."

"And well he should be. He's been without work far too long, and engraving headstones is a needed thing." Sadie's tone had become more serious. "I think it'll provide you and Luke with a good living and a job he shouldn't have to worry about losing."

"I hope so. If it were any other time of the year, I might be more comfortable with the idea of Luke traveling and being away from home. If only it was spring or summer. Then, too,

I'd have more to keep me busy outside in the warmer weather, like gardening and yard work, so I could keep my mind off Luke being gone." Meredith sighed deeply. "I just wish he didn't have to travel in this cold, snowy weather."

"I'm sure he'll be fine, and you will be, too, Meredith," Sadie said with a wave of her hand. "Those bus drivers know how to handle their vehicles in all kinds of weather. You have to remember they're trained for that."

Meredith nibbled on her lower lip as she looked out the kitchen window at the snow. "That's what my friend Dorine said, too."

Sadie slipped her arm around Meredith's waist. "Just give your worries to the Lord, like the Bible says we should do."

"I'm trying to do that, Sadie." Meredith managed a weak smile. "I think I'll feel better once I know Luke has arrived safely at his uncle's place. Then I'll just have to get through a few weeks before he comes home. There are days when I think I'll be able to handle it and then other times when I get really scared just thinking about it."

"Would you like to stay here with us while Luke is gone? You can bring Fritz along, too."

"I appreciate the offer, but I'm sure I'll be fine at home. I've already started a to-do list and plan to use the time he's away to get some things done that I've been wanting to do. Keeping busy will be my remedy for loneliness." Once Meredith found out whether she was pregnant, she planned to clean and organize the room that would become the baby's nursery. But no way was she going to share her suspicions with Luke's mom about being in a family way. Not until she'd told Luke.

"Keeping busy should help," Sadie said, pushing her glasses back in place. She lifted the lid on the pot of potatoes, poked them with a fork, and turned off the stove. "You know, in the forty-seven years Elam and I have been married we've never been apart for more than a few days."

"Really?"

"That's right, and the few times we were apart was because Elam had to go away on business when he owned the bulk food store."

Sadie carried the kettle over to the sink and poured the water out. "But even during those times it wasn't so bad, because I had our *kinner* to keep me company. Of course, all the boys missed Elam, and everyone was glad when he returned home."

Meredith sighed. "I'll be glad when Luke gets back from Indiana."

"Of course you will. Elam and I will be, too. With him being our youngest son and the only one living here in Bird-in-Hand, we're kind of partial to him." Sadie chuckled. "Course we love all five of our sons. It's just that we feel a bit closer to Luke."

"Is someone in here talkin' about me?" Luke asked as he and Elam entered the kitchen. Fritz followed close behind with his nose in the air.

Sadie gave Luke a hug. "It's a mother's right and privilege to talk about her son whenever she wants." She reached down to pet Luke's dog. "Hey there, boy. I made something special for you to eat."

Fritz's short tail wagged enthusiastically. Luke grinned and gave Meredith a wink. She was glad he had such a good relationship with his parents.

⬥

"Sure is a nice clear night," Luke said as he and Meredith walked hand in hand toward their house later that evening. In his other hand he held a battery-operated lantern to light their way. "Would you like to sit out on the porch awhile and look at the stars like we used to do when we were courting?"

"That sounds nice. I'll fix some hot chocolate for us to enjoy as we watch for falling stars."

"Sounds good to me. Would you like me to help?"

"No, that's all right, I can manage." Meredith motioned to the wooden bench that Luke had made last summer. "Just take a seat and relax. I'll be back in a few minutes."

"Okay." When Meredith went inside, Luke set the lantern on a small table, took a seat, and pulled the collar of his jacket up around his neck. It might be a clear night, but it sure was chilly. *Maybe I oughta go inside and get a blanket we can wrap up in,* he thought.

Luke was almost to the door when it opened suddenly and Meredith handed him a small quilt. "Thought we'd probably need this," she said, smiling at him.

"Guess we're thinking alike 'cause I was about to come inside and get one myself."

"I'll be back with the hot chocolate soon."

When she disappeared into the house, Luke took a seat and stared up at the sky. Ever since he was a boy he'd enjoyed watching the stars. It was fun to look for the Big Dipper and all of the other constellations. The night sky was beautiful with the bright moon and billions of twinkling stars.

Luke was also captivated seeing airplanes whiz across the sky. If he was looking in the right spot, occasionally he'd see a satellite move silently across the night sky. *I can't even imagine what it's like to be up in the sky like that, looking down at the earth,* he thought.

Early on in their courtship, Luke had told

Meredith how interested he was in flying and how he'd often wished he was a bird. He'd laughed when Meredith said she was keeping both of her feet on the ground, where they belonged. Luke knew he'd probably never get the opportunity to fly because taking trips by plane wasn't allowed in their Amish community. But it gave him something to daydream about.

Interrupting Luke's musings, Meredith reappeared, this time carrying a tray with two mugs of hot chocolate.

"Oh, good, I see you didn't forget the marshmallows," Luke said, grinning at her.

"Of course not. I know how much you love marshmallows." Meredith set the tray on the table and handed Luke a mug. Then she wrapped her fingers around the second mug as she sat down beside him. "I heated the milk extra hot, so you'd better sip it slowly at first," she cautioned.

He placed the quilt across both of their laps. "Are you warm enough, Merrie?"

"I'm fine. The hot chocolate will help warm our insides, too."

They sat in quiet camaraderie, drinking their hot chocolate and watching the stars, as a hoot owl serenaded them from one of the trees in their yard.

Meredith giggled.

"What's so funny?" Luke asked, blowing at the steam rising from his mug.

"You have melted marshmallow right there." Meredith pointed to his upper lip.

Luke laughed and swiped his tongue over the sweet-tasting foam.

"I probably have some marshmallow on my face, too." Meredith snickered and licked her lips. "Wow, the stars are so vivid tonight," she said, pointing above. "Oh, look—there's a falling star, Luke."

"I'm not superstitious, but I've heard it said that a falling star is a sign of good luck and that seeing one means something good's about to happen."

"We need something good to happen, all right," Meredith said.

"Guess we'd better not stay out here too much longer, though. I'll need to pack in the morning so I'm ready to go when my driver comes in the afternoon to take me to Lancaster to catch the bus." Luke reached into his pants pocket and pulled out his gold pocket watch. *"Die zeit fer ins bett is nau."*

Meredith sighed. "I don't want it to be time to go to bed yet. Just a little while longer, Luke. I'm not quite ready for the night to end."

"I know. I'd like nothin' more than to sit out here with you, watching the stars clear into the wee hours of the morning, but unfortunately, it's not an option. Not if I want to be awake and fully functioning in the morning."

"Could we sit for a few more minutes?" she asked.

"Jah, okay, but just a few." Luke was excited about his new venture, but he felt a bit edgy about things, just as his wife probably did. Tomorrow was a new beginning, but they'd also be saying goodbye. Even just a temporary separation made the situation that much harder for him.

"Mom said she invited you to stay with them while I'm gone," Luke said as Meredith snuggled closer. "Do you think you should take her up on that offer?"

Meredith shook her head. "I'll be fine here by myself, Luke. I'll have the pup, and I don't want you to worry about me, okay?"

He nuzzled her neck with his cold nose. "I won't, if you promise not to worry about me."

She gave no reply.

"Merrie, do you promise?"

"I'll try not to worry," she finally said. "I'm going to try and do as your mamm suggested and put my trust in the Lord."

He leaned over and kissed her cheek. "Now that's the kind of talk I like to hear from my fraa."

They sat awhile longer, reminiscing about their courting days. Although tonight was special, being on the porch in the quietness of the dark, it was hard not to think about what tomorrow would bring. It was strange, but Luke felt the same sense of loneliness as he imagined the hooting owl must be feeling—listening and waiting for an answer from its mate.

$\mathcal{C}$ HAPTER 5

$\mathcal{M}$ eredith sighed as she put the last of Luke's clothes in his suitcase and closed the lid. She wished he wasn't leaving for Indiana. She wished she could talk him out of going. But all the wishing in the world wouldn't change a thing, and it was pointless to keep dwelling on it.

Wiping sweaty hands down the front of her dress, she moved over to the bedroom window. The once-clear morning sky had turned gray, with thickening clouds, a heavy mist, and temperatures hovering near freezing, which could easily cause the roads to ice up. It appeared, from what she'd read in this morning's newspaper, to be the leading edge of a storm front—perhaps a major one. Why today, of all days, when Luke would be traveling, did the weather have to turn sour? This only fueled Meredith's anxiety over him leaving. Yesterday's weather was most likely the "calm before the storm."

Dear Lord, please keep Luke safe, she prayed. *Let this trip be the right decision for our future.*

"What are you thinkin' about, Merrie? You looked like you were a million miles away," Luke said, stepping up behind Meredith and slipping his arms around her waist.

"Oh, I was just thinking how much I'm going to miss you," she admitted, leaning back into his warm embrace and resting her head on his shoulder.

"I'm gonna miss you, too, but I'll be back before you know it."

Not wanting him to know how anxious she felt, she turned and smiled when he kissed the side of her face. "I know it won't be long, and I don't want you to worry about me while you're gone."

"I won't 'cause my folks, as well as yours, will be checking up on you, and knowing that gives me comfort. Seth also said if you need anything to let him know. Oh, and don't worry about the bad *wedder*, either," he said, moving away from the window and lifting his suitcase from the bed, "because I'm sure it won't cause any problems for the bus."

Meredith gave a nod, knowing it would do no good to say anything more to Luke about the weather. She couldn't control or change it, so it was going to do whatever it did anyway. She'd just have to pray for the best, take each day as it came, and try not to worry.

Commit each day to the Lord, she reminded herself. *And trust Him in all things.*

"Do you want me to pack you something to eat for the trip in case you get hungry?" Meredith asked as she followed Luke down the stairs. "How about I make up some ham and cheese sandwiches, and if you like, I could put in a couple of those Red Delicious apples we got at the market last week."

"I appreciate the offer, but after that big breakfast you fixed me this morning, and then the hearty chicken soup and homemade bread we had for lunch, I doubt that I'll feel hungerich for the rest of the day."

Meredith gave his stomach a gentle poke. "You might be full right now, but I'm sure it won't last for your entire trip. My guess is you'll be hungry before you reach Philadelphia."

"Well, if I do get hungry, I can buy a little somethin' to eat in Philadelphia or one of the other stops along the way." He wiggled his eyebrows playfully. "Besides, I'm so excited about this trip that I'm not even thinkin' about food. I just want to get there, learn all I can from Uncle Amos, and get back home to my beautiful fraa as soon as possible."

Meredith's cheeks warmed. She blushed way too easily—especially when Luke complimented her looks.

Just then, a horn tooted from outside. Luke went to the living-room window and looked out. "My driver's here, Merrie. It's time to go."

Meredith, wishing for a little more time with Luke, blinked against the tears threatening to escape. She wouldn't give in to them, though—at least not until after Luke had gone.

Luke pulled her into his arms and gave her a gentle kiss; then he picked up his suitcase and opened the door. "I did one more check around the house and didn't see anything that might cause you any problems," he said. "Oh, that big tree out back has a few limbs that should be taken off. They're hanging over the top of Fritz's pen, but the tree is good and healthy, and the branches aren't dead, so they should be fine till I come home. When I get back, I'll take care of trimming those branches." Luke hesitated, reaching out to gently rub Meredith's arm. "Well, it's now or never—I've gotta go."

Meredith forced a smile. Luke's concern for her needs made her cherish him all the more. Draping a shawl over her shoulders, she followed him onto the porch. "Don't forget to call me when you get there," she said, swallowing against the lump in her throat.

"I will, and remember—don't worry." Luke gave her one final hug and started across the yard.

Woof! Woof! Fritz raced back and forth, bumping his snout against the chain-link fence of his kennel. *Woof! Woof! Woof!*

That poor pup doesn't want to see his master go any more than I do, Meredith thought.

Luke stopped then walked over to the kennel. Reaching his hand through the fencing, he squatted down to bid farewell to his faithful friend. "It's okay, boy. I wasn't gonna leave without tellin' you goodbye," he said, giving Fritz's head a couple of pats. "Take good care of Meredith while I'm gone, and I'll see you in a couple of weeks."

Who says dogs aren't smart? That dog of ours sure is. Meredith smiled, despite the impending tears. Watching the way Fritz was acting, anyone could tell that he sensed Luke was leaving.

The dog continued to bark and jump at the fence as Luke turned and approached his driver's car. Just before he opened the car door, Luke looked back one more time and waved at Meredith. "Don't worry, Merrie. It'll all work out!"

She placed one hand against her stomach, while waving with the other, as the car drove away from the house. It took all her willpower not to run after Luke and beg him to stay. She stood watching as the vehicle pulled out onto the road and disappeared into the frigid mist. As she remained on the porch, looking at the spot where Luke had stood only moments ago, the fog moved in, enveloping her in its chilling mist.

Meredith wasn't ready to say goodbye yet, but then, would she ever have been ready for that? A forlorn feeling overwhelmed her, and as if walking in wet cement, her feet dragged toward the empty house.

Inside, the silence from her husband's absence nearly consumed her. It seemed as dreary and lonely in the house as it was outside with the cold, foggy mist. Grabbing the small quilt folded neatly on the couch,

Meredith wrapped herself in it and went to the rocker. All she wanted to do was blot out the hollowness that penetrated her soul, seeping in little by little, surrounding her like a cocoon. It was silly to feel this way, but saying goodbye to Luke had been even more difficult than she'd imagined.

Pushing back the despair with a feeling of anticipation, Meredith thought about the new life she hoped was growing within her. She wondered once more if she should have told Luke her suspicions about carrying his child. Well, it was too late now; he was gone. If it was true, he'd learn about it once he got home. It was news that could only be shared with him face-to-face—not over the phone after he arrived at his uncle's place. Oh, how she wished Luke could be with her tomorrow when she saw the midwife.

Come on now, snap out of it, Meredith told herself, drying her eyes and swallowing past the lump in her throat. *I'm a doer, and I'm going to get through this all right.* She had known beforehand that the parting would be difficult, but now that Luke was gone, she needed to move forward and look ahead. She rubbed her hand over the front of her dress. If she was pregnant, the baby would be the link holding her close to Luke, and it would help get her through the long days until his return. Not only that, the preparations for a new baby would keep her busy. She was ambitious and organized and couldn't wait to get started once her pregnancy had been confirmed. If her calculations were correct, she was about three months along.

Meredith was excited about the prospect of being a mother. She wasn't nervous like some women were when expecting their first child. After all, she and her sister Laurie had lots of practice helping their mother when their younger brothers and sisters were born.

Meredith smiled in eagerness, knowing that when Luke returned they'd quite possibly have two things to celebrate—his new business venture and the news that she was carrying their first child.

❦

Norristown, Pennsylvania

Staring out the window as the bus pulled out of Norristown, Luke felt as dismal as the foggy mist that seemed to envelop everything around them. At least so far the roads hadn't been icy. After hearing a few of the passengers talk about the weather, Luke knew they were headed toward the center of the storm as it came in from the west. Although the weather had been calm yesterday, it had changed overnight. But even now, it wasn't nearly as bad as the meteorologists predicted it would be.

Fidgeting on the cushioned seat to find a more comfortable position, Luke leaned in toward the window and thought about his beautiful wife. He regretted the stressful days he and Meredith had spent arguing about unimportant things and felt guilty for not letting her get the paint for the spare bedroom. What would it have hurt? After all, a few cans of paint wouldn't cost that much. Not even as much as his bus ticket had. Painting the room would have given Meredith something to do while he was gone and would have helped the time pass more quickly. Luke knew how she loved doing little projects that improved their home.

When I call Meredith after I get to Uncle Amos's place, I'm gonna tell her to go ahead and buy that paint, Luke decided. *I'm sure she'll be pleased about it, and since I'll be making money again soon, we can surely afford a few cans of paint.*

❧

Philadelphia

Alex Mitchell was on the run. He was hungry, cold, and in desperate need of a fix.

Crouched in an alley near the bus station, Alex peered around the Dumpster he'd been hiding behind for the last twenty minutes. With the exception of a mangy-looking cat watching him from atop the Dumpster, there was no sign of anyone or anything out of the ordinary.

Alex glared back at the cat, wondering how many more dirty critters like this there were in Philadelphia. He'd read in a newspaper not long ago that in the city of New York alone there were more than five hundred thousand stray cats. He figured there was close to that many here.

Maybe I've ditched those creeps who've been after me, he thought, forgetting about the cat and taking another look up the alley. *Better sit tight for a while longer, though, just in case they saw me run in here.*

Lately, it seemed all Alex did was look over his shoulder. He never forgot the day a certain drug dealer had said to him, "You'd better watch your back at all times, 'cause you never know who might be after you."

Who would have thought that Alex would end up on the run for what seemed like forever and a day? Alex could feel his body rebelling against the lifestyle he'd chosen, but he was powerless to do anything about it. The last time he'd looked in a mirror, he'd been shocked at the image looking back at him. Dark circles stood under his eyes, his cheeks were sunken, and his once-thick brown hair had thinned. He looked a lot older than his twenty-two years.

Alex had developed a cough recently, too, and as had been happening for so many days, another round of spasms seized his chest. Each racking cough made it hard to catch his breath, and after a while, his lungs felt as if they would explode. He coughed so loud it even scared the cat. Watching the mangy animal dart up the alley, he clamped his hand over his mouth to try to stifle the sound. If he didn't stop hacking soon, anyone looking for him would have no trouble knowing right where he was.

As Alex sat on his haunches, the coughing finally subsided. He shivered from the penetrating cold as his mind traveled through his past. He dredged up old memories of hiding like this from his drunken dad and remembered how fearful he'd been of the beating that would come if his old man discovered where he was.

Alex had shivered back then, too, but it wasn't from the cold. He would hope, and sometimes even pray, that his so-called father would grow tired of looking for him and pass out from his drunkenness before finding and beating him with a thick leather belt. Sometimes Alex got his wish. When he didn't, for days afterward he dealt with the pain of the stinging red welts left on his skin. His bum of a father needed someone to lash out at— especially after Mom ran off with some guy she'd met at the restaurant where she'd waited tables. Alex had only been ten years old when she'd split, and his older brother Steve was twelve. He had another older brother and two older sisters, as well, but as soon as they'd turned eighteen, they'd left, never to return.

It was bad enough that Alex's dad was the way he was, let alone having had a mom who hadn't stuck around to look out for him and his brother. If there was a God, which he seriously doubted, why then didn't He save Alex from this kind of life? What had he ever done to deserve all the misery he'd gone through?

Goodbye *to* Yesterday

Alex shifted his position as more memories flooded his mind. Back then, he'd longed for a real family—one like most of the other kids at school had. He often wondered what it would be like to have parents who'd paid attention to him and got involved in what he was doing. It was true he had two parents, Fred and Dot Mitchell, but that's where it ended. They'd held the status of being married, but really they were just two people who seemed to get some kind of enjoyment out of screaming, fighting, and making each other miserable. During the rare times when it seemed his folks might be getting along, they would often turn the tables and start yelling at Alex and Steve, ordering them around and constantly telling them what to do. To make matters worse, they seemed to get even more pleasure from reminding Alex that he never did anything right. Yes, they'd all lived under the same roof, but they were never a real family. When Alex's mother left, any hope there might have been about them becoming a true family unit vanished, just like the shabby cat that had hightailed it up the alley a few minutes ago.

Alex grimaced. School had never been fun for him, either. He remembered playing hooky each year on Parent/Teacher Day, when parents were invited to visit the classroom. Alex would leave the house as usual, making it look as if he were going to school, but halfway there, he would turn toward the woods and spend the day hidden among the trees until it was time to go home. No way was he going to invite his mom or dad into school and let them embarrass him in front of his peers. Neither was he going to sit in class being the only one who hadn't invited his folks. It was easier to avoid the whole scene altogether.

Alex avoided a lot back then, mostly to hide his bruises. He'd had one good friend for a short while, but that didn't last because Rudy moved away. After that, Alex didn't try to make friends. It was easier, because Alex trusted no one. Anyone he ever got close to left anyway, so what was the point? Even Alex's one and only pet dog had run off.

It wasn't great before Mom left, but

their household turned from bad to worse afterward, and soon his brother Steve started smoking marijuana. Not long after that, Alex tried it, too. By the time he was sixteen, he was doing more drugs and had dropped out of school. Then, tired of his dad's abuse and in need of money for his addiction, he'd hightailed it out of there, landed a job, and never gone back. Alex's obsession with marijuana wasn't enough, however, and in no time, he was doing the hard stuff—cocaine, heroin, and meth.

Doing and dealing drugs had been a part of Alex's life for so many years, he didn't know any other way to live. Now he was in over his head, just barely holding on. He'd stolen money from a couple of cocaine dealers, spent it on meth, and had no way to repay it. So the dealers were after him, and if he didn't escape, when they caught him they'd make sure he was dead.

Alex's life was in a downhill spiral; he was in a hole he couldn't crawl out of. What he needed was a break, a chance for freedom, an opportunity to start over in some other place. He doubted, though, that the chance would ever come. And if it did, what kind of a life would he choose?

As a child, loneliness, heartache, and pain had been all Alex knew. Now as an adult, anger replaced the longings of a little boy. He was suspicious of everybody and trusted no one. He doubted anyone would trust him, either, especially the way he looked. Just like his soiled clothes, he felt dirty. And with the fury behind his eyes and multiple scars and needle marks on his arms, he would make anyone uneasy.

Alex slowly shook his head. *I have no one left.* He had no idea where his brother Steve had ended up, either, or if he'd ever see him again. For all he knew, his older brothers and sisters could have disappeared off the face of the earth. Long ago, he'd given up any hope of having someone care about him. At this stage of the game, he'd probably spend the rest of his life alone and on the run—that is, if he lived long enough.

ℰ HAPTER 6

Bird-in-Hand, Pennsylvania

ℳ eredith glanced at the clock on the kitchen wall. It was half past six, and she wasn't even hungry. It was hard to think about supper when her husband wasn't here to share the meal with her. It was hard to think about anything other than wondering how Luke was doing on his journey so far. She figured he would be in Philadelphia around eight thirty and would be there until shortly after midnight. The bus would go to Pittsburgh for another transfer and wouldn't arrive in South Bend, Indiana, until six thirty Wednesday evening. Oh, how she looked forward to Luke's phone call, letting her know he'd arrived safely.

Woof! Woof! Woof! Fritz's frantic barking pulled Meredith's thoughts aside.

She glanced out the kitchen window and saw a horse and buggy coming up the lane. As the rig drew closer, she realized it belonged to her parents.

Meredith hurried to the door and stepped onto the porch just as Dad pulled his horse and buggy up to the hitching rail.

"Wie geht's?" Mom called as she made her way through the snow and approached the house.

"I'm fine but feeling kind of lonely," Meredith admitted after Mom joined her on the porch. "Luke left for Indiana this afternoon, and I already miss him."

Mom gave Meredith a hug. "That's why your daed and I stopped by—to see if you might come home with us tonight."

"I appreciate the offer," Meredith said as they entered the house, "but I'll be fine here by myself." She pointed to the window, where Fritz was jumping at the kennel fencing while frantically barking. "Besides, I have the pup to keep me company."

Mom rolled her eyes. "Like Luke's *hund* is going to offer you any companionship out there in his dog run."

"If I get lonely, I'll bring him in. Fritz is used to being in the house in the evenings, anyhow. I believe that dog thinks he's our protector, and frankly, I'm just fine with that, especially now that Luke is gone," Meredith explained. "So how's Laurie doing with those dolls she's been making to sell at the farmers' market?" Laurie was Meredith's nineteen-year-old sister, and growing up, they had been close because they were only three years apart.

"She's doing okay, but the dolls don't seem to be selling as well as they did when she first started making them. I guess it's due to the struggling economy," Mom said with a sigh.

"Well, at least she's keeping busy making the dolls," Meredith said.

"That's true, but she spends a lot of her free

time on them, and I worry that she's missing out on what should be the carefree days of her youth."

"It's good that Laurie's doing something she likes, and I'm sure she wouldn't do it if she didn't really enjoy the work." Meredith smiled. "So how would you and Dad like to join me for supper? I have some leftover soup in the refrigerator, and I'll make ham and cheese sandwiches to go with it."

"It's nice of you to invite us," Mom said, removing her shawl and black outer bonnet, "but Laurie and Kendra are cooking supper tonight, and it should be ready by the time we get home." She gave Meredith's arm a gentle squeeze. "We'd hoped you'd be coming home with us and would stay there until Luke gets home."

"I can't do that, Mom. I have things to do here. The horses need tending, and so does Fritz." Meredith sighed deeply. *Why is she bringing this up again? Doesn't she think I'm capable of staying alone?*

"Your brother can come over to feed and

water the horses, and if you like, Fritz can come over to our place with you. The kinner have become attached to him since you and Luke got married—especially the younger ones." Mom smiled. "And if I know Laurie and Kendra, they'll probably fix the dog some special treats. Ole Fritzy boy will be one spoiled pooch if you stay at our house."

"I'm sure that whatever my sisters fixed would be good," Meredith said, "but Fritz and I are going to stay here while Luke is gone. I want to be available when he calls and leaves a message letting me know he got to his uncle's safely."

Just then, Dad entered the room. "Are you comin' home with us?" he asked, looking at Meredith.

She shook her head. "I appreciate the offer, but I'd prefer to stay here."

Dad looked over at Mom and said, "This daughter of ours is an eegesinnisch one, jah?"

Mom nudged his arm. "And where do you think she gets that stubborn streak from?"

Dad chuckled. Then he turned back to

Meredith and said, "We accept your decision to stay home alone, but if you need anything, don't be afraid to ask."

"I appreciate that." Meredith gave her parents a hug. "Danki for stopping by. I was glad for the visit."

"It wasn't much of a visit. Least not for me," Dad said with a wink.

Meredith smiled. For a man of fifty-four years, her dad was in tip-top health. His arms were still muscular from all the farmwork he'd done over the years, and Meredith found comfort in his warm embrace. Just like when she was little, Meredith felt safe whenever Dad was around.

"Now don't you forget," Mom said, slipping her black bonnet back on her head, "just let us know if you need anything."

Mcredith smiled. "I will."

Once her parents had gone, the house was quiet again, so Meredith busied herself and turned the propane stove on low to slowly heat up the soup. While that was getting warm, she decided to go upstairs and take a quick look at the spare room to see what might need to be done in preparation for a baby.

Leaning against the doorway, Meredith looked around. It was a nice-sized room, with a smaller closet than hers and Luke's, but there was plenty of room for baby furniture. *In just six short months, this could actually be our baby's room,* she thought, smiling.

Meredith's lips compressed. As eager as she was to paint this room, she didn't want to go against Luke's wishes, so if she was pregnant, the painting could wait to be done until after he got home. She was sure he'd have no objections once the news was shared with him as to why she was so eager to paint.

"I guess the first thing I need to do is go through all these boxes and take some things up to the attic," Meredith said, thinking out loud. "That way, I'll have more room in here and can plan what we'll need for the baby and where to put everything."

Continuing to look around, she could almost visualize the crib along one wall and the baby's dresser and a few other things on the other wall. Unless she found another rocking chair at an auction or sale, Meredith would use the one in the living room and maybe ask Luke to bring it up to the baby's room once the time drew closer for her to deliver. One thing was for sure: the rocker would go right by the window.

Meredith closed her eyes and could almost feel their tiny baby nestled in her arms and sleeping quietly as she rocked the precious bundle. Placing one hand over her stomach, she wondered if she might be carrying a boy or a girl. That would be the joy Luke and she would share when the baby was born. Meredith knew it was possible to find out before the baby came, whether it was a girl or a boy, but she wanted to be surprised and knew that Luke would most likely agree. As she was sure all parents felt, she didn't mind what it was as long as the baby was healthy. It seemed good to have a plan, and once she had confirmation from the midwife that she was expecting a baby, Meredith would start clearing out this room.

Back downstairs, Meredith hummed while

she stirred the soup, enjoying the aroma of sweet corn and chicken broth. Meredith was getting hungry, and the hot soup would taste good.

With the motion of the bus, Luke's eyes were getting heavier, and his head bobbed each time he caught himself nodding off. If he kept this up, he'd have a stiff neck by the time he got to the City of Brotherly Love. He was already missing Meredith and thinking she had probably finished supper by now.

I wonder what she made tonight, he thought. Just thinking about a home-cooked meal caused his mouth to water. The bus would be arriving in Philadelphia soon, and when it did, Luke planned to get something to eat.

Probably should have let Meredith fix me those sandwiches to bring along, he thought with regret. *Guess I oughta listen to her more often. One of those delicious ham and cheese sandwiches would sure stop my stomach from rumbling right now.*

Luke's thoughts were halted when the elderly man across from him began to snore. He sounded like an old bear growling. The fellow's snoring was louder than Luke's stomach rumbling. Even some of the other passengers on the bus turned toward the man and snickered.

Guess I can't fault him for that. According to Meredith, I snore, too. Luke smiled just thinking about it. *Course, I don't have to listen to myself.* He tried not to laugh, but the old man's nasal rumblings sounded so funny. By now, the snoring had gone up a notch, reminding Luke of a buzz saw. *Surely,* he thought, watching the man, *my snoring can't be as bad as that. If it is, then I'm sure Meredith would have teased me about it.*

Luke removed his black felt hat and placed it in his lap. Then he leaned his head against the back of the seat and closed his eyes. He figured he may as well get a little sleep while he could, and hopefully he wouldn't snore. One snoring person on the bus was enough. Since the bus wasn't full, he was able to stretch out into the empty space beside him.

Luke couldn't quit thinking about

Meredith. By now, she probably had Fritz inside with her for the night. That gave him some measure of comfort. As the bus rolled toward Philly, the last thing Luke thought about before drifting off to sleep was a prayer for Meredith's safety while he was gone.

Meredith had just finished cleaning up the kitchen and was thinking about getting ready for bed when she remembered that she'd forgotten to bring Fritz inside. She hated to go out in the dark, frigid weather, but it wouldn't be fair to let him stay out in the kennel all night, and she'd never be able to sleep, knowing he was out there in a cold doghouse, while she was warm and comfortable inside. Luke had put plenty of straw inside Fritz's shelter, but it wasn't like being in the house where it was warm and more comfortable. Meredith was mad at herself for not bringing Fritz in sooner, or even asking her dad to bring him in when he and Mom were here. But Meredith had so much on her mind, she'd forgotten all about the pup.

Bundling up in one of Luke's heavy jackets, Meredith grabbed a flashlight and went out the back door. As the cold air hit her cheeks, she breathed deeply, inhaling the scent of her husband from the coat that encompassed her. Meredith closed her eyes and could almost imagine Luke standing there holding her.

The wind had begun to blow, and it was snowing again. Meredith was sorry she hadn't thought to put on her boots. Her feet were soaking wet already and turning colder with each step she took. She shivered and made her way as quickly as possible to Fritz's dog run.

Woof! Woof! Fritz wagged his tail when Meredith approached the fence.

"Are you ready to come into the house, pup?" Meredith asked, opening the gate.

Woof! Fritz dashed out of the dog run, raced across the yard, leaped onto the porch, and started pawing at the back door.

Meredith chuckled. "I know just how you feel."

After they got inside, she kicked off her shoes and put on a dry pair of socks. Neither she nor the dog wasted any time heading into the living room. Meredith stoked up the fire then went to her rocker and picked up the Bible on the small table beside her. Fritz curled up on the braided rug next to the fireplace.

Opening her Bible to a place she had marked with a ribbon, Meredith read a verse of scripture she thought was especially meaningful and had underlined some time ago. "Thou wilt keep him in perfect peace, whose mind is stayed on thee: because he trusteth in thee." Isaiah 26:3.

Meredith smiled and felt herself relax. God's Word always had a way of speaking to her just when she needed it the most. For the moment at least, she felt sure that, despite all her worries, everything concerning her and Luke would turn out fine.

ℰHAPTER 7

Philadelphia

ℒuke was glad to be off the bus for a while. He needed the chance to walk around and stretch his legs. He'd slept most of the way and had ended up with a kink in his neck, just like he'd figured he would.

Luke felt the side of his head, amazed that there weren't any bumps. He'd hit the window so many times from his head bobbing around, it was surprising that he'd even been able to get in a few winks.

He pulled out his pocket watch to check

the time. The bus he'd be transferring to in Philadelphia wouldn't be leaving the station until 12:20 a.m., which meant he had plenty of time to get a bite to eat and buy a newspaper so he'd have something to read. Luke was always interested to see what was going on in the rest of the world and wanted to check for any articles on the weather to see if the storm had reached the areas where he'd be traveling.

Before putting the watch back in his pocket, he clicked it shut, remembering what a great gift it was that Meredith had given him this past Christmas. How she'd ever found that particular pocket watch was amazing. Etched on the outer lid was a bird dog that looked just like Fritz. It was the perfect gift. Rubbing his thumb over the etching made his heart lurch. He was already homesick—for his wife, his dog, and even his horse. Luke felt like an outsider in this busy place and longed for the simple things of home.

As Luke stood on the curb looking both ways, he spotted a diner near the bus depot. The place looked inviting, and with his stomach growling and the wonderful aromas coming from the diner, he was drawn in that direction. When he stepped into the restaurant, he found a stack of newspapers on a rack near the door. He took one, paid the cashier, and then found a seat in a booth near the window, with the bus depot still in view. He noticed a tear in the vinyl seat cover, and as he looked around, Luke noticed the café was a bit run down, but the place was clean and crowded. That could only mean one thing: the food must be good.

When the waitress came, Luke ordered a ham sandwich, fries, and a glass of chocolate milk. Waiting for his food to come, he read the newspaper, while all around him, people came and went. This sure was a busy place. There was an old jukebox in the corner, and someone had chosen a tune where the singer was crooning, "You were always on my mind." Luke wasn't used to hearing that kind of music, but he couldn't help listening to the part of the song that said, "Maybe I didn't treat you quite as good as I should have." The song was kind of catchy, that was for sure, but all it did was make Luke regret even more how he'd treated Meredith recently.

Trying to block out the words in the song, he stuck his nose deeper into the paper and concentrated on what he was reading. It was hard to believe all the bad news, and he searched through several pages before he found something positive to read. A group of senior citizens had participated in a class called "Water Walking," which gave them the exercise they needed, while getting to know other people their age.

Luke smiled at the happy looks he saw on the faces of the elderly people in the picture. They obviously enjoyed being in the water, just as he did during the warm summer months. If he had an indoor pool to use, like these people did, he'd probably swim in it all year.

He also found an article on the winter storm that had already created havoc in states to the west. It sounded like his travels would be taking him right through the blizzard. Even so, his excitement about his new job opportunity outweighed any anxiety about bad weather.

Luke's thoughts turned to Meredith once again and the fact that he'd soon be able to provide a decent living for their future. Luke could never repay his uncle for the gratitude he felt for giving him a chance for a new beginning.

Earlier in the evening in an act of desperation, Alex had stolen some drugs. Now he had not one, but two dealers after him. But even in his most desperate times, he still had bouts of luck. In the alley behind the bus station he'd found a five-dollar bill, so he'd ducked into the diner across the street to get something to eat. He would figure out what to do from there.

Taking a seat, he drummed his fingers nervously along the edge of the table. He was exhausted, cold, and wanted something to eat almost as much as he'd needed his last fix. He looked around while he waited, hoping he wasn't too conspicuous. The place was sure busy and bustling with people. Alex was so hungry he could eat a horse and was almost to the point where he felt faint.

"What'll it be?" the middle-aged brunette waitress asked, looking down at Alex without a hint of a smile.

"What'll five bucks get me?" he mumbled, rubbing his hands briskly over his bare arms, wishing he looked a little more decent.

"How about a burger and some chips?" she replied stiffly, making no eye contact with him.

"Yeah, that's fine."

"You want some water to wash it down?"

"Sure." Alex nearly choked, trying to hold back his irritating cough.

When the waitress went to turn in his order, Alex sat back and surveyed his surroundings. Over the years there'd been a few instances when people were nice to him, but most of the time they acted like the waitress, either looking at him with disgust or avoiding his gaze altogether. Alex didn't care anymore. There wasn't a person on this earth who meant anything to him.

Now there's a familiar scene, Alex thought when he spotted an old man slouched in a booth near the door. The guy's eyes were closed, and his mouth hung open as his head lulled against the back of the seat. *The lazy bum's probably drunk.* Alex clenched his jaw. *Reminds me of my old man when he was in one of his stupors. Sure don't need no reminders of them horrible days. Just wanna forget about my past and try to have some kind of a future. But if I don't get outa here before I get caught, that's not likely to happen.*

Directly across from Alex sat a young bearded man with blond hair, reading a newspaper. He wore dark trousers and a heavy-looking black jacket. A black felt hat lay on the table next to his plate of fries.

Alex pulled his fingers through the ends of his own bristly beard, noting that the man's beard was about the same length as his. After closer observation, he realized the guy was Amish. Alex had seen some Amish men at the farmers' market in Philly, selling their wares. Just a week ago, Alex had stolen some produce from one of their stands. The old guy had been so busy yakking with one of his customers that he hadn't noticed what Alex had done. Or if he had, he'd chosen not to say anything about it.

Alex's burger came about the time the Amish man was finishing up with his meal, and when the fellow took his wallet out to pay, Alex couldn't help but notice the wad of bills sticking out. He also noticed how nice the waitress was to the bearded man as she counted back the change he was due. *What's the point of bein' nice to people? They're all strangers anyways, and they don't care about nobody but themselves.*

Alex gave his beard a quick tug. *I'll bet that guy would be an easy target.* From what little Alex knew about the Amish, he understood them to be a peaceful bunch of folks. He figured it shouldn't be too difficult to get what he wanted from the man. He just needed the right opportunity.

ℰ CHAPTER 8

Bird-in-Hand, Pennsylvania

ℳeredith rolled over onto her side and bunched up her pillow. She'd been in bed nearly two hours and hadn't been able to sleep because she couldn't turn off her thoughts. She'd started nodding off while reading downstairs, but by the time she'd gone to the kitchen for a glass of milk and then climbed the stairs to her room, she was wide awake again. All Meredith could think about was how much she missed Luke. She wished he'd let her pack some sandwiches for his trip. At least he'd have something from home in his stomach right now. *I wonder where he ended up eating and what kind of food he had.*

She glanced at the battery-operated clock on the small table beside her bed and saw that it was getting close to midnight. Luke was probably in Philadelphia by now and should be boarding the next bus soon. Meredith tried to imagine everything as if it was playing out in front of her, but all she could do was guess. The trip to Indiana was long, and Luke would be glad when he got there. Being patient wasn't easy, but she'd have to wait for his call tomorrow evening to find out how his journey had gone.

Lying on the small braided rug near the foot of Meredith's bed, Fritz woke up suddenly and started to bark.

"What's the matter, pup? Do you need to go out?"

Fritz darted around to her side of the bed and put one paw on her chest. *Woof! Woof!*

"Oh, all right." Meredith pushed the covers aside and climbed out of bed. Slipping into her robe and slippers, she went downstairs and let the dog out.

"Now hurry up and do your business," Meredith called as Fritz dashed into the yard. The frigid air made her even more awake, so she quickly shut the door. Spring couldn't come too quickly. She looked forward to planting her garden and tending all the colorful flowers in their yard. She loved having the windows open and the front and back door, too. The mild spring air wafting through the house always made everything smell so fresh and clean, especially after a good rain.

Several minutes went by; then Meredith heard a—*Thump! Thump!*—on the door, followed by a loud bark. "Are you ready to come in?" she asked, opening the door.

Woof! Woof! Fritz tromped inside and raced up the stairs.

When Meredith entered the bedroom, she found Fritz sitting on the floor at the foot of her bed, whining.

"I know, pup," Meredith said, patting the dog's head. "Luke hasn't even been gone a full day, yet I miss him so much."

Then, seeing the wet paw prints on the

floor, she grabbed a towel and wiped up the water.

Going around in circles until he found just the right position, Fritz grunted and finally bedded down on the floor.

Meredith crawled into bed, and as she pulled the covers up to her chin, she said a prayer on her husband's behalf. It seemed like she'd been praying for Luke a lot since he'd left this afternoon.

But that's okay, she reminded herself. *In 1 Thessalonians 5:17 we are told to pray without ceasing.*

<hr />

Philadelphia

Alex gulped down half of his burger and grabbed the rest of it in a napkin. Then he slapped his money on the table and followed the Amish guy out the door. When he saw the fellow enter the bus station across the street, his interest increased. He had no idea where the guy might be heading, but anyplace out of Philly would be good enough for Alex. Wanting a quick getaway, and to be far from the drug dealers he'd stolen from, he thought this might end up being a piece of cake. To have the money he needed would be an extra bonus.

Leaning into the wind, and giving in to yet another coughing fit, Alex stepped inside the bus station, grateful for the warmth. *Sure wish I had a jacket,* he thought.

Once again, his gaze went to the Amish man, who had taken a seat between two old men on the other side of the room. The lucky guy had a jacket and a hat to chase away the cold. All Alex had was a dirty old T-shirt and a pair of faded, holey jeans. If he switched clothes with this fellow, he'd finally be warm.

I'll bet the guy won't give me too much trouble, Alex thought. *If he's peaceful, like I've heard the Amish are, then he oughta do everything I ask.*

He took a seat on the bench across from the Amish man and gave a nod when the fellow glanced his way. There were too many other people in the bus station for him to make a move right now, but if he could get the guy alone, he might have a chance. Feeling a bit stronger with some food in his belly, Alex decided to finish his burger and wait the man out.

After eating, then sitting there waiting, Alex felt himself getting drowsy, but he wouldn't give in to the temptation to sleep. As more passengers departed, the bus depot started clearing out. Alex knew for sure that his luck was changing when the Amish man stood and headed for the restroom. He could make his move now. Getting to his feet, he didn't hesitate to follow, anxious to get this over with.

Luke had just finished washing his hands when the scruffy-looking bearded man he'd seen come into the bus station shortly after he had entered the restroom. He stood staring at Luke a few seconds then sidled up to him and said, "Gimme your clothes."

Luke's forehead wrinkled. "You. . .you want my clothes?"

"That's what I said. Give 'em to me right now!" The man's hand shook as he balled it into a fist. "You'd better do as I say, or you'll be sorry."

Luke was tempted to resist, but seeing the desperation on the man's face, he thought better of it. This would be a good opportunity to show his Christianity. And with nothing but a T-shirt and a pair of holey jeans, the poor man was probably cold. Luke knew he could borrow some clothes from his uncle when he got to Indiana. Besides, he'd be getting on the bus soon, and that would give him some warmth.

But the scruffy-looking fellow wasn't satisfied with just Luke's clothes. Once they'd traded, he demanded Luke's wallet. Luke could see that the man was shaky and agitated, so he offered to buy him something to eat.

"Already ate," the man growled. "Now, don't give me no trouble! I just want some money, and I want it right now!"

Luke shook his head, determinedly. It was one thing to give up his clothes and put on the stranger's uncomfortable jeans and dirty T-shirt, which didn't smell too good. He couldn't simply hand over his wallet. He needed that money to give his uncle as a down payment for the equipment he'd need to begin his new business. He had to somehow convince this determined fellow to change his mind about the money.

"I won't give you my wallet," Luke said, holding his ground and hoping to intimidate the angry-looking man. Luke had never met anyone like this before, and he hoped the situation would be resolved peacefully but feared it wouldn't. Maybe someone would walk into the restroom, and the encounter would be over before it got any worse.

"And I say you will hand it over!" the man shouted, his eyes squinting and his face turning red.

That determined expression and rising temper caused Luke to realize he was in serious trouble. Short of a miracle, this would be anything but a nonviolent encounter.

The look of outrage in the fellow's eyes gave no hint of him wavering, either, and before

Luke could protect himself, the man stepped forward and punched him in the stomach, causing Luke to double over from the pain. Unleashing his fury, and with a string of curses, the enraged man knocked Luke to the floor and began viciously kicking him everywhere, including his head and face. Over and over, Luke was beaten, until he didn't think he could take any more pain. He tried to protect himself, but everything inside of him felt like it was breaking, and he was sure his body couldn't take much more abuse.

Dear God, please help me, Luke silently prayed as another serious blow connected to his head.

Will I ever see my beautiful fraa again? he wondered. Then everything went black.

ABOUT THE AUTHOR

New York Times bestselling author, Wanda E. Brunstetter became fascinated with the Amish way of life when she first visited her husband's Mennonite relatives living in Pennsylvania. Wanda and her husband, Richard, live in Washington State but take every opportunity to visit Amish settlements throughout the States, where they have several Amish friends. Wanda and her husband have two grown children and six grandchildren. In her spare time, Wanda enjoys photography, ventriloquism, gardening, beachcombing, stamping, and having fun with her family.

Visit Wanda's website at www.wandabrunstetter .com, and feel free to e-mail her at Wanda@ wandabrunstetter.com.

THE SAGA CONTINUES IN

The
SILENCE *of*
WINTER

COMING MARCH 2013!

OTHER BOOKS BY WANDA E. BRUNSTETTER

Adult Fiction

The Half-Stitched Amish Quilting Club

KENTUCKY BROTHERS SERIES
The Journey
The Healing
The Struggle

BRIDES OF LEHIGH CANAL SERIES
Kelly's Chance
Betsy's Return
Sarah's Choice

INDIANA COUSINS SERIES
A Cousin's Promise
A Cousin's Prayer
A Cousin's Challenge

SISTERS OF HOLMES COUNTY SERIES
A Sister's Secret
A Sister's Test
A Sister's Hope

BRIDES OF WEBSTER COUNTY SERIES
Going Home
Dear to Me
On Her Own
Allison's Journey

DAUGHTERS OF LANCASTER COUNTY SERIES
The Storekeeper's Daughter
The Quilter's Daughter
The Bishop's Daughter